THE STORY OF THE
UTAH
JAZZ

CREATIVE EDUCATION

Published by Creative Education
123 South Broad Street
Mankato, Minnesota 56001
Creative Education is an imprint of The Creative Company.

DESIGN AND PRODUCTION BY **EVANSDAY DESIGN**

PHOTOGRAPHS BY Getty Images (Bill Baptist / NBAE, Cosmo
Condina, Scott Cunningham / NBAE, Tim Defrisco, Stephen Dunn,
Focus on Sport, Noah Graham / NBAE, Otto Greule / Allsport,
Andy Hayt, Keystone Features, NBA Photo Library, Chuck Pefley,
David Sherman / NBAE, Jeff Reinking / NBAE, Rick Stewart,
Rocky Widner / NBAE)

LIBRARY OF CONGRESS CATALOGING-IN-PUBLICATION DATA

LeBoutillier, Nate.
The story of the Utah Jazz / by Nate LeBoutillier.
p. cm. — (The NBA—a history of hoops)
Includes index.
ISBN-13: 978-1-58341-427-9
1. Utah Jazz (Basketball team)—History—
Juvenile literature. I. Title. II. Series.

GV885.52.U8L43 2006
796.323'64'09792258—dc22   2005051772

First edition

9 8 7 6 5 4 3 2 1

COVER PHOTO: *Deron Williams*

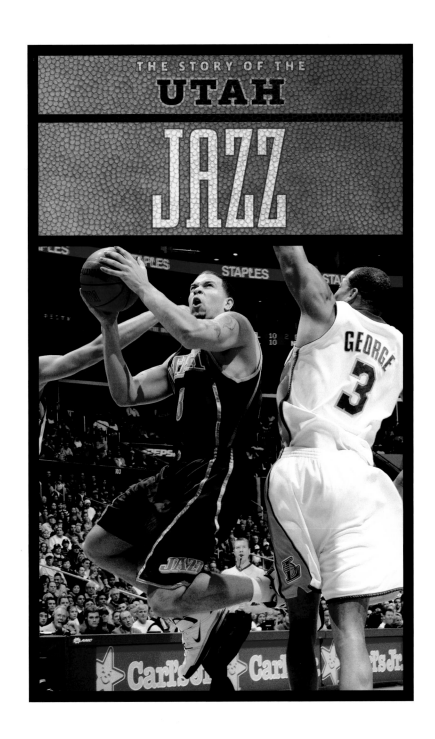

THE STORY OF THE

UTAH

JAZZ

NATE LeBOUTILLIER

CREATIVE EDUCATION

StocktontoMalone.

IT SHOULD'VE BEEN JUST ONE WORD.

WITH THE PRECISION OF A FINELY TUNED MUSICAL
INSTRUMENT, THE UTAH JAZZ'S KARL MALONE AND JOHN
STOCKTON MADE THEIR OWN BEAUTIFUL ON-COURT
MUSIC. AS STOCKTON DRIBBLED, LULLING HIS DEFENDER
TO SLEEP, MALONE WOULD APPROACH AND, LIKE A
STONE WALL, SET A PICK ON STOCKTON'S DEFENDER.
THEN STOCKTON WOULD BURST INTO MOTION, RUBBING
SHOULDERS PAST MALONE, WHO PIVOTED TOWARD THE
BASKET TO RECEIVE A PERFECT PASS FLICKED FROM
STOCKTON'S HANDS. TO THE RIM MALONE WOULD CHARGE,
POWERING THE BALL INTO THE BASKET. THE STOCKTON-TO-
MALONE PICK AND ROLL WAS CLASSIC JAZZ BASKETBALL.

UTAH JAZZ
Salt Lake City Utah

THE BEGINNINGS OF JAZZ

1

AT FIRST GLANCE, SALT LAKE CITY, UTAH, HAS virtually nothing in common with New Orleans, a swinging Louisiana city known for its jazz music and many nightclubs. Yet both cities have been home to the same National Basketball Association (NBA) team. That team, born as the New Orleans Jazz, moved to Utah's quiet capital in 1979 and became an instant hit.

9

The Jazz were born in the early 1970s in New Orleans, a colorful city famous for its music and carnivals

1974

Famous basketball showman "Pistol" Pete Maravich entertained Jazz fans in both New Orleans and Utah

NBA JAZZ

The Jazz started out in New Orleans in 1974. The team's owners were determined to make the Jazz like New Orleans itself—colorful and entertaining. To do this, they decked out their team in bright uniforms of purple, green, and gold. They also brought in one of the league's greatest showmen by trading for point guard Pete Maravich.

Known to fans as "Pistol Pete," Maravich was a sensational player whose speed and flair for ball handling were unmatched. "This man is quicker and faster than [NBA stars] Jerry West or Oscar Robertson," said Atlanta Hawks forward Lou Hudson. "He gets the ball up the floor better. He shoots as well. Raw talent-wise, he's the greatest who ever played."

Maravich put on some flashy shows in New Orleans—even leading the NBA in scoring with 31 points per game in 1976–77—but the team struggled, posting losing records in its first three seasons. Despite the strong play of forward Leonard "Truck" Robinson, guard Gail Goodrich, and center Rich Kelley, the team missed the playoffs again in 1978 and 1979. A knee injury slowed Maravich down, and New Orleans fans grew impatient with the struggling team. With attendance at home games shrinking, the team's owners decided to move the Jazz to Salt Lake City in 1979.

NIGHT OF THE SMOKING PISTOL

Pete Maravich loved to score points and make the game look pretty. On February 15, 1977, "Pistol Pete" went to an extreme. In a game against the New York Knicks, the Jazz star scored 48 points before the fourth quarter had even begun. A teammate told him, "You better get a new firing pin, Pistol, 'cause you're wearing that one out." But Maravich kept on firing. He scored 20 more points in the fourth quarter for a franchise record of 68 points, the most ever by a guard in the NBA until the Chicago Bulls' Michael Jordan scored 69 in 1990. After the game, a 124–107 victory, Pistol Pete wasn't completely satisfied. "I could have scored more," Maravich said. "I missed a lot of easy shots early in the game."

DANTLEY FINDS A HOME IN UTAH

THE PEOPLE OF UTAH WERE NO STRANGERS TO professional basketball. In the late 1960s and early '70s, Salt Lake City had been home to the Utah Stars of the American Basketball Association (ABA). The Stars franchise folded in 1975. Four years later, Utah fans welcomed the Jazz to town.

13

Despite being one of the NBA's shortest forwards, 6-foot-5 Adrian Dantley attacked the basket fearlessly

JAZZ

The Jazz honored Darrell Griffith, a sharpshooting star of the 1980s, by retiring his jersey number

BULL

The Jazz were determined to get off to a better start in Utah than they had in New Orleans. Tom Nissalke was hired as head coach, and Frank Layden—a big man known for his sense of humor—was named the team's new general manager. One of Layden's first moves was to trade for 6-foot-5 forward Adrian Dantley. Dantley had been named the NBA Rookie of the Year in 1977, and in the seasons that followed, he became one of the league's top scorers. "There's no one player in the league who has shown me yet he can handle Dantley," Coach Nissalke said. "You can't stop him inside."

No one could stop Dantley in 1979–80, as the forward led the Jazz with 28 points per game and was named an NBA All-Star. After the season, Utah made another major roster change, releasing Maravich. But the team soon got a boost from high-flying young guard Darrell Griffith, an excellent shooter. As Layden once said, "Griffith could shoot from the shores of the Great Salt Lake and probably make it."

Still, the Jazz continued to lose, and in 1981, Nissalke was fired as head coach and replaced by Layden. In 1983–84, Utah soared to a 45–37 record and made the playoffs for the first time. Dantley led the NBA in scoring, Griffith continued his hot shooting, point guard Rickey Green led the league in steals, and 7-foot-4 center Mark Eaton blocked an NBA-high 351 shots. These players led Utah to solid records again the next two seasons, but the Jazz never truly contended for the league championship.

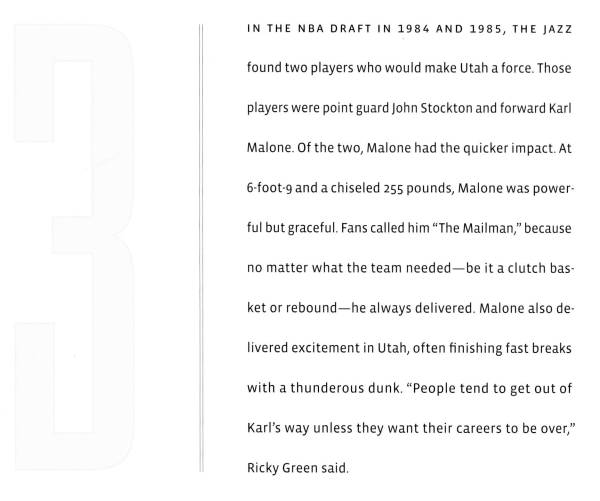

3

IN THE NBA DRAFT IN 1984 AND 1985, THE JAZZ found two players who would make Utah a force. Those players were point guard John Stockton and forward Karl Malone. Of the two, Malone had the quicker impact. At 6-foot-9 and a chiseled 255 pounds, Malone was powerful but graceful. Fans called him "The Mailman," because no matter what the team needed—be it a clutch basket or rebound—he always delivered. Malone also delivered excitement in Utah, often finishing fast breaks with a thunderous dunk. "People tend to get out of Karl's way unless they want their careers to be over," Ricky Green said.

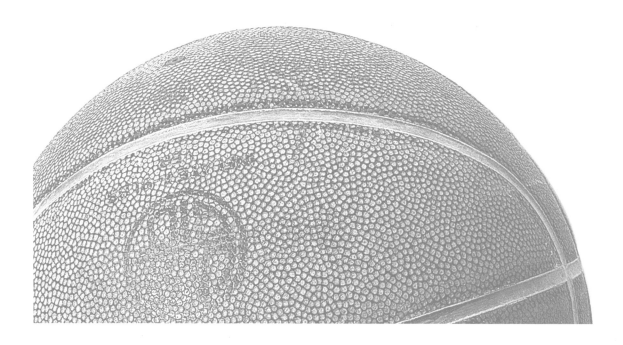

17

Despite his weightlifter's physique, Karl Malone showed astounding speed in running on fast breaks

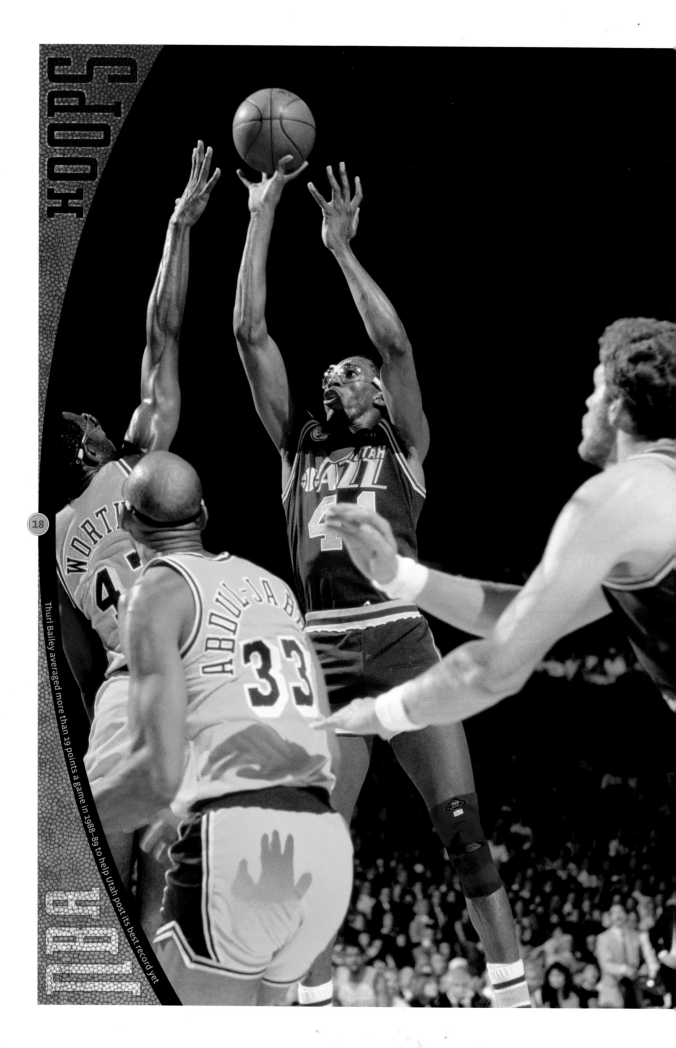

NBA

Thurl Bailey averaged more than 19 points a game in 1988-89 to help Utah post its best record yet

In 1986, the Jazz decided to make Malone their cornerstone player and traded Dantley to Detroit. The Mailman immediately assumed command in Utah, leading the team with 21 points and 10 rebounds per game in 1986–87. In 1987–88, Stockton emerged as a star as well. That year, the 6-foot-1 guard led the NBA in assists with nearly 14 per game. Stockton rarely turned the ball over and almost always put his passes to teammates right on the mark.

During the 1988–89 season, Layden stepped down as Utah's coach and promoted his top assistant, Jerry Sloan, in his place. Behind Sloan, Stockton, and Malone, the Jazz emerged as one of the Western Conference's best teams in the late 1980s and early '90s. From 1988–89 to 1991–92, Utah won more than 50 games every season. But the playoffs were a different story. Even with the addition of such players as guard Jeff Malone and forward Thurl Bailey, the Jazz were knocked early from the playoffs every year.

The first half of the 1990s continued as the '80s had ended. The Jazz posted winning records every year, but they fell short of the NBA Finals each postseason. During those seasons, Stockton and Malone continued to secure their legacy as two of the game's greatest players.

In 1990–91, Stockton handed out an NBA-record 1,164 assists. In 1994–95, he surpassed Los Angeles Lakers star Magic Johnson as the league's all-time assists leader. "I think it's great to play with a guy like John Stockton," said Malone. "I don't know if I can describe what he's meant to my career. Playing with a point guard who truly wants to get his teammates involved before himself—you don't find that much in this league anymore."

BIG MARK EATON

When Cypress (California) Junior College basketball coach Tom Lubin found a 7-foot-4 giant working underneath cars in a mechanic's jumpsuit in the late 1970s, he couldn't help wondering what he'd look like in a basketball uniform. Lubin convinced Mark Eaton to play, and the rest was history. Eaton went on to play for the Jazz from 1982 to 1994 and was twice voted NBA Defensive Player of the Year. After back problems forced him to retire, the feared shot-blocker opened a successful Italian restaurant in Salt Lake City in 1996. "After traveling for so long (with the Jazz), I knew what I didn't like," Eaton said. "I can't say I knew everything about the restaurant business, because I didn't. But I knew what I didn't care for, and that was bad food and bad service."

21

JAZZ

Few teammates in NBA history played together as long—or as well—as John Stockton and Karl Malone

THE JAZZ RISE

4

IN 1995–96, WITH THE HELP of SHARPSHOOTING guard Jeff Hornacek and rugged forward Antoine Carr, Utah cruised to a 55–27 record. It then powered through the playoffs to reach the Western Conference Finals for the third time in five years. Playing against the Seattle SuperSonics, Utah lost the series in seven close games.

For years, critics had said that the Jazz were bound to fall off their winning pace, but Utah only grew stronger. In 1996–97, The Mailman poured in 27 points per game and was named the NBA's Most Valuable Player (MVP), and the Jazz rolled to a 64–18 record—their best mark ever. In the playoffs, they crushed the Clippers and Lakers to reach the Western Conference Finals. This time, the Jazz would not be denied, beating a tough Houston Rockets team to advance to the NBA Finals at last.

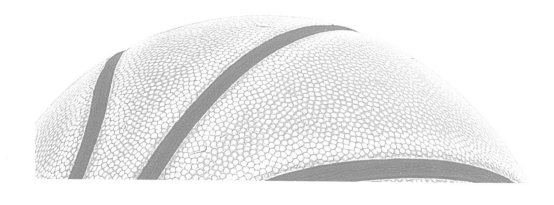

23

JAZZ

Brilliant outside marksman Jeff Hornacek led the Jazz in three-point shooting in five different seasons

Although he made few headlines, Greg Ostertag was a valuable rebounder and shot-blocker

In the Finals, the Jazz faced the Chicago Bulls and star guard Michael Jordan. The Bulls won the first two games, but Utah battled back to even the series at two games apiece. Stockton and Malone repeatedly ran their trademark pick and roll play, and young players such as forward Bryon Russell and center Greg Ostertag made big contributions. But Jordan dominated in the next two games to lead Chicago to its second straight NBA championship.

A year later, Utah charged right back to the NBA Finals to meet the Bulls. The result was identical. With Utah on the ropes in Game 6, Malone scored 31 points. Jordan was even better, however, netting 45 points in the final game of his Bulls career and sinking the winning shot with six seconds remaining to give Chicago the title again.

LONG-TERM SLOAN

With the most coaching wins in Jazz history, Jerry Sloan has solidified a name for himself in the record books. The gritty, emotional coach was an equally intense player. As a guard for the Chicago Bulls in the 1960s, Sloan backed down from no one. "In his first year with us, he led the league in floorburns and fights in practice," joked Sloan's Bulls coach, Red Kerr. After Sloan's playing career was over, he still couldn't get the game out of his blood. The Bulls figured his fiery leadership would be a good thing to have on their bench, so they made him head coach in 1979, but Sloan lasted only three seasons. He moved on to Utah and guided the Jazz to the NBA Finals in 1997 and 1998, only to lose to—who else?—the Bulls.

THE JAZZ PLAY ON

AFTER LOSING IN THE FINALS FOR THE SECOND straight year, many fans wondered if Utah would replace Stockton or Malone with younger talent while the veterans still had trade value. But Jazz president Frank Layden made clear that he intended to keep the team's veterans together for as long as it took. "We want to have statues of John and Karl outside the Delta Center someday," he said. "You'll never see us panic or make changes just to make changes. We do things differently here."

Malone proved that age had not slowed him by winning the league's MVP award again in 1998–99, and Stockton's hustle continued to pace the offense. The pair led Utah to the playoffs every year they played for the Jazz, but after the 2002–03 season, the long marriage ended. Stockton retired, and Malone played 2003–04 with the Los Angeles Lakers before retiring at season's end.

27

In 2003–04, forward Andrei Kirilenko led all Utah players in scoring, rebounding, steals, and blocked shots

28

Jazz fans hoped that 6-foot-11 forward Mehmet Okur, a native of Turkey, would become an inside force

After the loss of their longtime stars, the Jazz looked to new talents such as Andrei Kirilenko, a 6-foot-9 forward from Russia. Other young players such as forward Kris Humphries and big men Mehmet Okur and Carlos Boozer also joined the mix, and in the 2005 NBA Draft, the Jazz found their point guard of the future: Deron Williams. Said the brilliant passer from the University of Illinois, "I'm just honored to play for the Jazz and to play after John Stockton, to wear the same jersey he wore and be on the same floor he was on."

Although the Jazz suffered their first losing season in 20 years in 2004–05, folks around the NBA don't expect the Jazz to stay flat for long. The legendary John Stockton and Karl Malone combination rewrote the Utah playbook—all future Jazz players simply need to read and practice it to make beautiful basketball.

WHAT'S IN A NAME?

The name for Utah's basketball team—"Jazz"—doesn't seem quite right. The state of Utah is known as a quiet, religious region, and its capital and largest city—Salt Lake City—is the worldwide headquarters of the Church of Jesus Christ of Latter-day Saints, also known as the Mormon Church. Today, Mormons still make up most of Utah's population. Jazz, on the other hand, is the soulful, lively musical invention of the Deep South. The name fit the team when it started out in New Orleans, the so-called birthplace of Jazz, but it seems a little out of place in Utah. The people of Utah may not play a lot of jazz music, but they certainly love their Jazz. From 1991–92 to 2000–01, the Jazz averaged more than 19,000 fans per home game.

FUNNYMAN FRANK LAYDEN

Frank Layden served the Jazz as team president, general manager, and head coach, remaining a cornerstone of the organization for more than 20 years. The once fat man weighed 335 pounds in the 1980s but trimmed down to 160 after he quit coaching in 1988. Layden was well-known for his sense of humor. He once joked about his heaviness, "I stepped on a scale that gives fortune cards, and the card read, 'Come back in 15 minutes. Alone.'" Once, when a fan asked him what time the game started, he cracked, "What time can you be there?" But perhaps what Layden was known best for was his common practice of shooting baskets in the dark, alone, a grown man pretending he was an NBA star. Layden always said, "You have to make life fun."

JAZZ

A hardworking forward with star potential, Kris Humphries was part of Utah's new generation of talent

31

INDEX